When Duck Got Stuck

For Lauren -
May you always have a love of nature,
and our natural environment. x

WHEN DUCK Got Stuck

Written by Joanna Watts

Illustrated by Jess Bircham

As the warm summer breeze twitched
Pru's whiskers, Lou raced down the hill.
"Woo hoo," she shouted.

PIPPINDIDDY
WOOD

"Where shall we go today?" said Lou.

Pru stretched. "Miaow."

"Alright — let's go to our favourite place," said Lou.
And off they went.

Lou was swinging ... but Pru was sniffing.

"What are you looking for, Pru?" said Lou.

Lou crouched down and peeked into the bush.

Scared and in pain, the duckling quacked and quivered.

"Oh no – you're hurt," said Lou. "But we're going to help you."

"There — that's better, you're all untangled now," said Lou.

The duckling hobbled at first, but soon was flapping!

Suddenly there was rustling in the bushes, and out came Mother Duck.

Lou watched Pru race off with astonishing speed.

"We weren't hurting your duckling," called out Lou.

But it was no use, the chase was ON!

Back through the wood they went.

Under the swing ... over the bridge ... through the trees and around the lake ... before FINALLY coming to a stop.

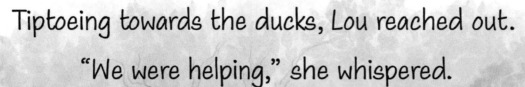

Tiptoeing towards the ducks, Lou reached out.

"We were helping," she whispered.

Lou coaxed Pru down and gave her a big hug.

"You see?" she told Mother Duck. "We all need help sometimes."

The duckling chirped happily. Mother Duck

realised they were friends.

Lou picked up the rubbish while Pru played in the thick leaves. With a swish of her tail and a bat of her paw, she revealed more rubbish for Lou to collect.

What a team!

Lou squashed it all into the basket ...

leaving just enough room for Pru.

Lou decided to make a sign for visitors to read.

She chose the one that turned out best.

"Where shall I put it?" said Lou.

Pru miaowed loudly.

"Yes, that's the perfect spot," agreed Lou.

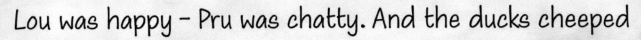

Lou was happy – Pru was chatty. And the ducks cheeped and chirped with joy!

Creatures big and small
call this wood their home
Don't leave mess and rabbish
So they are safe to roam

When you've finished playing
Take a look around
Make sure all you leave behind
Are footsteps on the ground

Creatures big and small
call this wood their home
Don't leave mess and rubbish
So they are safe to roam

When you've finished playing
Take a look around
Make sure all you leave behind
Are footsteps on the ground

As she said goodbye to her new feathered friends,
Lou gathered up her things. Pru yawned.

"Ok," said Lou. "Let's go."

And she hopped back on her bike, and cycled home.

AUTHOR NOTE

Thank you so much for reading my story - I do hope you enjoyed it. I would love to receive your feedback, and would be extremely grateful if you posted a review on the platform from which the book was purchased.

Made in the USA
Middletown, DE
09 December 2021

54914668R00018